P9-AQS-949

It's Halloween, Dear Dragon

Modern Curriculum Press
BEGINNING
TO
READ
Series

It's Halloween, Dear Dragon

Margaret Hillert

Illustrated by Carl Kock

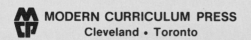

MODERN CURRICULUM PRESS
Cleveland • Toronto

JE

Text copyright © 1981 by Margaret Hillert. Illustrations and jacket design copyright © 1981, by Modern Curriculum Press, Inc. Original copyright © 1981, by Follett Publishing Company, a division of Follett Corporation. All rights reserved. No portion of this book may be used or reproduced in any manner whatsoever without written permission from the publisher except in the case of brief quotations embodied in critical reviews and articles. Manufactured in the United States of America.

Library of Congress Cataloging in Publication Data

Hillert, Margaret.
  It's Halloween, dear dragon.

  (MCP beginning-to-read books)
  SUMMARY: A boy and his pet dragon play in the autumn leaves, make a jack-o-lantern, eat pumpkin pie, dress in costumes, go trick-or-treating, enter a costume contest, and fly together.
  [1. Halloween—Fiction. 2. Dragons—Fiction] I. Kock, Carl. II. Title.
PZ7.H558It   [E]   79–23433

ISBN 0-8136-5524-2 (Paperback)

ISBN 0-8136-5024-0 (Hardbound)

1 2 3 4 5 6 7 8 9 10   88 87 86 85

NEW HANOVER COUNTY PUBLIC LIBRARY

MLib.

Look up here.
Do you see what I see?
Something red.
Something yellow.

And look down here.
We can play here.
This is fun.

6

7

See what I can do.
I can make you look funny.
Oh, oh, oh.
Funny, funny you.

I can work, too.
Work, work, work.
I can help Father.

9

Come here. Come here.
You can work, too.
You can help do this.

10

Now come with me.
I want to get something.
You can help.
Run, run, run.

Here is a big one.
We want this one.
And a little one, too.

13

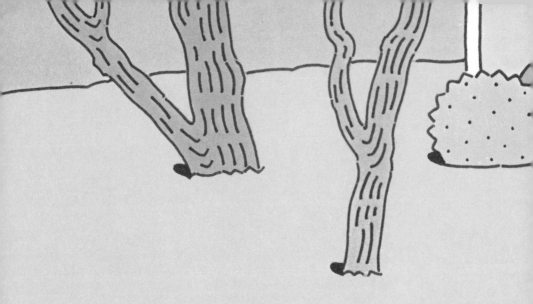

Father, Father.
Look what we have.
Can you help us make something?

14

15

I can. I can.
I can do it.
Look at this.
Do you like this?

16

And look at this one.
I can make it funny.
It looks like you.

17

18

Here, little one.
Come up here.
This is something funny.
Do you want to see this?

Mother, Mother.
Can you make something, too?
Can you make something for us?

Yes, I can.

I can make something good.

You will like it.　　　　21

Look at me.
See what I have.
Guess who I am.
Guess, guess.

We will get something here.
Something good.
We can eat it.
This is fun.

24

Not you.
Not you.
No, you will not do.

25

Here.
You are the one.
Here is something for you.
You are funny.

26

Oh, my.
What do I see?
What do you have here?

Look what we can do.
Away we go.
Up, up, and away!
What a good ride.

28

29

Here you are with me.
And here I am with you.
Oh, what a happy Halloween, dear dragon.

Margaret Hillert, author and poet, has written many books for young readers. She is a former first-grade teacher and lives in Birmingham, Michigan.

It's Halloween, Dear Dragon uses the 64 words listed below.

a	father	make	the
am	for	me	this
and	fun	mother	to
are	funny	my	too
at			
away	get	no	up
	go	not	us
big	good	now	
	guess		want
can		oh	we
come	Halloween	one	what
	happy		who
dear	have	play	will
do	help		with
down	here	red	work
dragon		ride	
	I	run	yellow
eat	is		yes
	it('s)	see	you
		something	
	like		
	little		
	look(s)		

NEW HANOVER COUNTY PUBLIC LIBRARY

3 4200 00058 1146

C

Y x

#1 Sto

JE   581146
hillert, Margaret
    It's halloween, Dear
dragon.

NEW HANOVER COUNTY PUBLIC LIBRARY
201 CHESTNUT ST.
WILMINGTON, NC   28401